dick bruna

miffy

SIMON AND SCHUSTER
London   New York   Sydney   Toronto   New Delhi

Mr and Mrs Bunny lived

in a white house all alone.

The house had scarlet shutters

and a garden of its own.

Mr Bunny grew the flowers.

He weeded, dug and sowed.

He watered all the flowerbeds

and watched the flowers grow.

Mrs Bunny cleaned the house

and kept it snug and neat

and then she'd do her shopping

from the shops along the street.

Look, she's bought some peapods,

so crisp and sweet and green

and a pear for Mr Bunny,

the best he's ever seen.

Mrs Bunny woke one night.

Her eyes popped open wide.

She thought, I'm sure there's someone there.

I heard a noise outside.

She tiptoed to the window.

She gasped and had to stare.

For standing in the garden

an angel waited there.

Now you shall have your wish, she said,

a baby will be yours.

She beat her wings and flew away

to her home among the stars.

And, sure enough, one lovely day

their little bunny came,

with ears so long and fur so white —

and Miffy was her name.

The cock and hen came by to see.

Their little chicks came too.

Even the cow was keen to look

at baby Miffy. Moo!

Hello, she mooed politely.

I see your baby's born.

But is she getting sleepy?

Did I see her yawn?

Yes, Miffy's head was nodding.

Her little eyes were closing.

Miffy needed dreamland

where soon she would be dozing.

So out crept cow and cock and hen

and chicks, without a cheep.

The shutters closed, the house grew quiet

and Miffy went to sleep.

Original title: nijntje
Original text Dick Bruna © copyright Mercis Publishing bv, 1963
Illustrations Dick Bruna © copyright Mercis bv, 1963
This edition published in Great Britain in 2014 by Simon and Schuster UK Limited
1st Floor, 222 Gray's Inn Road, London WC1X 8HB, A CBS Company
Publication licensed by Mercis Publishing bv, Amsterdam
English re-translation by Tony Mitton © copyright 2014, based on the
original English translation of Patricia Crampton © copyright 1995
ISBN 978 1 4711 2078 7
Printed and bound in China
A CIP catalogue record for this book is available from the British Library upon request
10 9 8 7 6

www.simonandschuster.co.uk